NINJA KITTIES™

ACTIVITY STORYBOOK

Kitlandia is in Danger!

Bee-Bee Believes in His Inner Strength

Created and illustrated by
KAYOMI HARAI

Story by
ROB HUDNUT

Happy Fox BOOKS

Kayomi Harai – Creator and Illustrator

Born in Osaka, Japan, Kayomi Harai is a self-taught artist who began drawing and painting at an early age. Her paintings are full of imagination and feature a wide range of animals, including cats, tigers, leopards, wolves, eagles, and dragons. She likes to use watercolors, colored pencils, and pastels in her artwork and creates art digitally also. Her works have been exhibited and licensed around the world. She currently lives in San Jose, California.

Kayomi created Ninja Kitties as a way to remind children that they can be anything they want to be and that they should always believe in themselves.

KITTY  **LALA**  **POPPY**

Kayomi was inspired by her three mischievous kitty assistants, who she adopted from a local animal shelter. The oldest is Kitty (a tortoiseshell tabby) and the babies are Lala and Poppy (calico sisters). They have been her inspiration and joy ever since the day she brought them home.

Rob Hudnut – Author

Rob Hudnut is an award-winning writer and storyteller in children's entertainment and the owner and founder of Rob Hudnut Productions, where he specializes in creating play- and faith-based franchises for kids. Some of their global clients include NBCUniversal, Alpha Toys, ICON Creative Studio, Kavaleer Productions, and more. Prior to starting his own production company, Rob was the executive producer and vice president of Mattel's entertainment division for 19 years, where his work included award-winning entertainment for Barbie, Hot Wheels, Fisher-Price Little People, Rescue Heroes, DC Superhero Girls, Masters of the Universe, and other Mattel brands. An Emmy-nominated songwriter, Rob also co-wrote the first Barbie movie, *Barbie in The Nutcracker*, and more than 50 songs for the Barbie movies, as well as songs for Hot Wheels and Fisher-Price.

NINJA KITTIES and related design marks are trademarks of New Design Originals and Kayomi Harai.

Ninja Kitties Kitlandia is in Danger! Activity Storybook
Copyright © 2022 by Kayomi Harai and Happy Fox Books, an imprint of Fox Chapel Publishing Company, Inc. All rights reserved.

Series Editor: Elizabeth Martins
Series Designer: Llara Pazdan

ISBN 978-1-64124-123-6

Library of Congress Control Number: 2021948399

To learn more about the other great books from Fox Chapel Publishing, or to find a retailer near you, call toll-free 800-457-9112 or visit us at *www.FoxChapelPublishing.com.*

We are always looking for talented authors. To submit an idea, please send a brief inquiry to acquisitions@foxchapelpublishing.com.

Fox Chapel Publishing makes every effort to use environmentally friendly paper for printing.

Printed in China
First printing

Additional image credits: pages 2, 3, and back jacket, top, yellow burst: starlineart, Freepik.com; page 9, frame around art: Giraphics, Shutterstock.com.

NINJA KITTIES

The Ninja Kitties are seven royal brothers and sisters who change from princes and princesses into super ninjas! Zumi, Sora, Leon, Bee-Bee, Drago, Mia, and Hana have all sorts of adventures and fun together.

Grandma Tabby is their trainer and used to be a Ninja Kitty. She has trained them in **NINJA GOODNESS**—kindness, confidence, love, empathy, individuality, and persistence. With the power of **NINJA GOODNESS** and their super Ninja Kitty gems, the Ninja Kitties protect Kitlandia! They must keep their gems from the Fang Gang—Winty Wolf and his two sidekicks, Cody Coyote and Jed Jackal—who will stop at nothing to steal the gems!

Zumi   SUPER LEAPER!

Zumi is the oldest kitty. She is super kind and smart. Zumi is a black belt super ninja, and she can jump super high!

Sometimes Zumi doesn't remember to listen. She also wants everything to be perfect. Her brothers and sisters help her remember to listen and include everyone's ideas.

Bee-Bee SUPER STICKY POWERS!

Bee-Bee is the funniest and stickiest Ninja Kitty! He can shoot honey from his paws and use his sticky power to climb walls. Bee-Bee also uses his sticky power to slow down the Fang Gang, fix things, or play a joke on his brothers and sisters.

Sometimes Bee-Bee doesn't believe in himself. Grandma Tabby and his brothers and sisters help him remember that his powers and gifts are special—just like he is!

Drago SUPER HEAT & GLOW!

Drago is one hot kitty! He has super heat and light power. His tail and ears light up with a powerful glow. He uses his power to light up the dark or heat things up.

Sometimes, Drago forgets how important it is to work as a team. He wants to do everything by himself. His brothers and sisters help him remember that they are stronger together.

Sora SUPER FLYER!

Sora can fly super fast! She can also fly high in the air and see any trouble in Kitlandia!

Sora loves to dress up and play, but she sometimes needs help remembering to share. It's a good thing her brothers and sisters are there to remind her!

Mia SUPER WATER POWERS!

Mia is a super water kitty! She can control water, especially water bubbles! She is a strong swimmer and loves a good wave!

Mia can sometimes get sad when she has trouble with her water powers. Grandma Tabby reminds her to never give up and to always try again!

Leon SUPER STRONG!

Leon is super strong and super silly! He also has a powerful lion roar!

Sometimes he leaps before looking and roars before thinking, but the other Ninja Kitties are always there to help him. Leon is the tallest, and he loves a good snack!

Hana SUPER FLORAL POWERS!

Hana is the youngest and smallest of all the Ninja Kitties. Her super plant power lets her grow any kind of plant or flower.

Hana is still learning to talk about how she feels. She is also learning to land on her paws out of the portal! It's hard to get her brothers and sisters to listen to her because she is the youngest. But when they do listen, they realize she has bright ideas!

King Reo and Queen Mira

King Reo and Queen Mira are the rulers of Kitlandia and the parents of the Ninja Kitties. They love their beautiful kingdom and everyone in it.

They are extra thankful that their kitties are the Ninja Kitties! Sometimes, King Reo forgets to keep his children's special powers a secret. It is a good thing Queen Mira is there to remind him.

Grandma Tabby

Grandma Tabby is the Ninja Kitties' trainer. She knows best about being a Ninja Kitty because she used to be one! Don't let Grandma Tabby's gray whiskers fool you—she can leap high in the air and has amazing ninja powers.

Grandma Tabby has given a ninja gem to each of her grandchildren. The power in the gems boosts the Ninja Kitties' powers. Grandma Tabby likes to read a book and drink a cup of tea when she isn't training the Ninja Kitties.

7

WINTY

JED

CODY

The Fang Gang

Winty Wolf, Cody Coyote, and Jed Jackal are the "Fang Gang" and are always up to no good. These three buddies are always making trouble and trying to steal the Ninja Kitty gems. Winty is the leader, and he has always wanted a Ninja Kitty gem. If only he had a bit of ninja power for himself! **NINJA GOODNESS?** More like **NINJA MAYHEM!**

Winty thinks that the Ninja Kitties are actually the royal kitties. No one sees that they look alike, but maybe he is on to something . . .

Kitlandia is in Danger!

It is a sunny day in Kitlandia.

Grandma Tabby calls the royal kitties to practice. Zumi, Bee-Bee, Drago, Sora, Mia, Leon, and Hana love training with their grandma!

The royal kitties shout **"NINJA GOODNESS!"** and spin around. Magic flows from the gems in their crowns. They turn into Ninja Kitties!

Zumi shows off her super ninja leap.

"Wonderful jump!" Grandma Tabby says.

"Ha! I've seen grasshoppers jump higher!" Bee-Bee says.

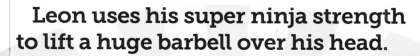

Leon uses his super ninja strength to lift a huge barbell over his head.

"Leon! You are so strong," Grandma Tabby says.

"Strong *and ticklish!*" Bee-Bee laughs.

He uses his ninja honey power to shoot honey at Leon's armpit. Leon *is* ticklish! He drops the barbell with a *CRASH!*

13

The crash surprises everyone! Hana falls from the magic vines she made. Drago trips. Mia drops the water ball she made.

The water ball pops and soaks all the kitties. Bee-Bee laughs hard. He laughs so hard that he doesn't see the puddle of honey on a bench and sits in it.

Leon is mad. "All right, Bee-Bee," Leon says, "let's see what you can do with *your* powers."

"That's easy," Bee-Bee says. He does not know that the honey has glued his bum to a bench. He tries to fly, but the bench goes up with him!

Bee-Bee pushes the bench off, but it makes him crash! His brothers and sisters laugh.

"That's it! I'm out of here!" Bee-Bee says. He runs off. As he runs, he changes back into royal clothing.

Bee-Bee looks out of the castle. Grandma Tabby comes up beside him. "I'm done being a Ninja Kitty," he tells her.

"Why is that?" Grandma Tabby asks.

"Because my brothers and sisters laughed at me," he says.

"Is that really the reason?" Grandma Tabby asks.

Bee-Bee looks up with tears in his eyes. "It's because they all have better powers than me!"

"You have great ninja powers," Grandma Tabby says. "Don't compare yourself to others. Seeing how your brothers and sisters use their powers can help you use your own powers better."

"But my powers aren't cool," he says. He runs off again.

Pepper the woodpecker flies into the training room. "Winty Wolf, Cody Coyote, and Jed Jackal are chopping down huge trees near the Emerald River!" he says. "The trees are falling into the water!"

"Where, Pepper?" Zumi asks.

"Near Diamond Dam," Pepper says.

"Go, go, go, Ninja Kitties!" Grandma Tabby says. "I don't know what the Fang Gang is up to, but it doesn't sound good."

"Where is Bee-Bee?" Hana asks.

"We'll be fine without him," Zumi says. She places a paw on the Kitlandia map. "To the Emerald River!" she says. The map turns into a magic portal. They jump into it.

The Ninja Kitties pop out of the portal and land near Diamond Dam. Hana is still trying to land on her paws!

The Fang Gang is sailing on a raft made of logs. The raft is heading right for the dam!

Winty Wolf is happy his plan worked! Cutting down trees made the Ninja Kitties come. Now, he can catch them and steal their gems.

Winty shouts to Cody and Jed. "Catch those kitties!" They pull out large nets and wait for the Ninja Kitties!

The Ninja Kitties need to stop Winty from crashing into the dam. Mia swims to the front of the raft. She uses her strong swimming kicks to try to slow it down.

Sora uses her ninja flying power to hold back the raft. Hana uses her ninja plant powers to wrap seaweed around the raft. But the river is too strong, and the raft is too heavy!

Cody and Jed sneak up on Mia and Sora.
"I have the blue one!" Cody yells.
"I have the purple one!" Jed shouts.
Mia and Sora are caught!

Zumi leaps and lands on Jed and Cody. Their nets go flying. Mia and Sora are free! Sora catches Mia, and a net lands on Winty!

"Can't you two do anything right?" Winty yells.

Leon and Drago are waiting to help on the dam. The raft smashes into the dam. Leon and Drago fall!

Leon almost falls into the river, but he grabs the edge of the dam. "Uh-oh!" he says. "The dam is going to break!"

Zumi shouts to Sora, "Get Bee-Bee!"

"Yes! We need Bee-Bee!" all the Ninja Kitties cry.

Sora flies to the castle.

Sora finds Bee-Bee playing checkers with Grandma Tabby. "Bee-Bee!" she says. "We need you at the dam!"

"Sorry," Bee-Bee says. "I'm not a Ninja Kitty anymore."

"But Bee-Bee," Sora says. "We need you and your powers!"

Bee-Bee looks at Grandma Tabby. He is not sure what to do.

"What does your heart say?" Grandma Tabby asks.

Bee-Bee thinks. Then, he stands up, spins, and says, **"NINJA GOODNESS!"** He turns to Sora and says, "Let's fly!"

Sora and Bee-Bee get to the dam.

"Bee-Bee!" Zumi says. "You are the only one who can fix the dam!"

"I'm on it!" he says.

Bee-Bee uses his ninja flying power and honey power to fill the cracks!

Bee-Bee works as fast as he can. He flies around the dam like a bee going from flower to flower.

"It's working!" Sora says. "Keep going, Bee-Bee!"

Zumi watches Bee-Bee. "Bee-Bee, you are a hero!" she cheers.

"Why you—" Winty says. The Fang Gang runs at Zumi, but she jumps up just in time. Uh-oh, Fang Gang!

Cody, Winty, and Jed land in the water far below. "Next time, those gems will be mine!" Winty yells.

In the Ninja Training Room, the Ninja Kitties are practicing their powers. Bee-Bee is cheering everyone on. "Great jump, Zumi! Wow, Leon, you are so strong! Nice water ball, Mia! Way to fire up, Drago! Super flying, Sora! Great plant powers, Hana!"

Bee-Bee stands proud and tall.

Just like Bee-Bee, you are perfectly YOU! There are things you can do that no one else can. Don't compare yourself to others. Remember to take time to learn from others, and be happy that you are special just as you are.

NINJA SCRAMBLE

Unscramble the words below! Hint: Some words are Ninja Kitty names!

1. OYLELW   _ _ _ _ _ _
2. HNOEY   _ _ _ _ _
3. EEBEBE   _ _ _ _ _ _
4. SROA   _ _ _ _
5. LOEN   _ _ _ _
6. NNIJA   _ _ _ _ _
7. IKTTY   _ _ _ _ _

See page 48 for the answer keys to Bee-Bee's puzzles.

CROSSWORD PAW-ZZLE

Test what you know about the Ninja Kitties!

WORD BANK

- BEE-BEE
- CHECKERS
- HANA
- HONEY
- LEON
- MIA
- PURPLE
- YELLOW

DOWN

1. What does Bee-Bee use to fill the cracks of the dam?
2. Which Ninja Kitty makes water balls?
3. What game does Bee-Bee play with Grandma Tabby?
6. What is Bee-Bee's favorite color?

ACROSS

4. Which Ninja Kitty makes magic vines?
5. Who saves Diamond Dam?
7. What color is Sora's ninja suit?
8. Which Ninja Kitty is super strong?

CRACK THE NINJA CODE!

Crack the code to see what Grandma Tabby has to say to Bee-Bee.

A	B	C	D	E	F	G	H	I	J	K	L	M
1	2	3	4	5	6	7	8	9	10	11	12	13

N	O	P	Q	R	S	T	U	V	W	X	Y	Z
14	15	16	17	18	19	20	21	22	23	24	25	26

__ __ __ __ __ __ ,   __ __ __ __
20 8 5 18 5 19   15 14 12 25

__ __ __   __ __   __ __ __ ...
15 14 5   15 6   25 15 21

__ __   __ __ __ __ __ __ __ __ !
2 5   25 15 21 18 19 5 12 6

43

DRAW & COLOR

Use the grid to draw Bee-Bee!

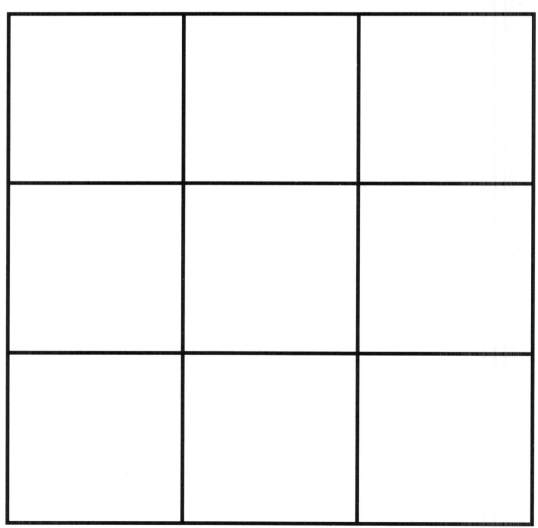

WORD SEARCH

Find the words in the grid below. Look across and down!

H	B	N	I	N	J	A	X	N	I
Q	E	H	B	O	H	O	N	E	Y
Q	E	V	L	K	E	W	C	Q	Z
M	B	F	L	Y	R	Y	A	P	H
L	E	L	Z	V	O	N	S	Y	H
D	E	B	P	F	K	I	T	T	Y
L	B	B	Y	C	A	S	T	L	E
Z	M	F	Z	L	W	I	N	T	Y

WORD BANK

- BEEBEE
- CASTLE
- FLY
- HERO
- HONEY
- KITTY
- NINJA
- WINTY

SPOT THE DIFFERENCE

Find 3 differences between the two pictures.

"BEE" YOURSELF!

Bee-Bee learns that he is special and that no one else is quite like him!
You are special, too! Write what makes you unique below!

_____

_____

_____

_____

_____

_____

_____

WHERE ARE THE NINJA KITTIES?

The Ninja Kitties are playing Hide-and-Seek in the Ninja Training Room. Pepper the woodpecker is looking for them! Can you help him find all seven of them?

ANSWER KEY

NINJA SCRAMBLE
Page 41

1. Yellow
2. Honey
3. Bee-Bee
4. Sora
5. Leon
6. Ninja
7. Kitty

CROSSWORD
Page 42

ACROSS
4. Hana
5. Bee-Bee
7. Purple
8. Leon

DOWN
1. Honey
2. Mia
3. Checkers
6. Yellow

CRACK THE CODE
Page 43

There's only one of you...
be yourself!

WORD SEARCH
Page 45

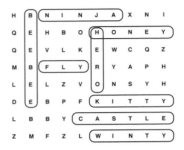

SPOT THE DIFFERENCE
Page 46

Antennae, Ninja Belt, Wings

SEEK AND FIND
Page 47

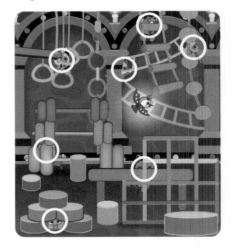

The Ninja Kitties are always ready for an adventure!
Start your own adventure with the Ninja Kitties using the stickers below!

Zumi
Super Leaper

Sora
Super Flyer

Bee-Bee
Super Sticky Power

Drago
Super Heat & Glow

Grandma Tabby

Hana
Super Floral Powers

Mia
Super Water Powers

Leon
Super Stong